LYNN REISER

NIGHT THUNDER AND THE QUEEN OF THE WILD HORSES

Greenwillow Books **New York**

Watercolor paints and a black pen were used
for the full-color art. The text type is Bembo.

Printed in Singapore by Tien Wah Press
First Edition 10 9 8 7 6 5 4 3 2 1

Library of Congress
Cataloging-in-Publication Data

Reiser, Lynn.
Night thunder and the Queen of the Wild
Horses / by Lynn Reiser.
        p.   cm.
Summary: A little girl and the Queen
of the Wild Horses seek the source of the
loud noises keeping them awake.
ISBN 0-688-11791-0 (trade).
ISBN 0-688-11792-9 (lib. bdg.)
[1. Sleep—Fiction.   2. Bedtime—Fiction.
3. Noise—Fiction.   4. Animals—Fiction.
I. Title.   PZ7.R27745Ni   1995
[E]—dc20   93-25734   CIP   AC

This is
Susan's
book.

One rainy night
a little girl felt lonely.
So she drew a wild horse.

She drew the Queen of the Wild Horses.

And then
she was sleepy.
It was bedtime.
So the little girl
yawned
and said
"Good night"
to
the Queen of the Wild Horses
and went
to sleep.

 Outside the night was dark,
and the night was wet,
and the night was quiet,
except for the patter of the rain.

CRASH

The little girl woke up.
The Queen of the Wild Horses woke up.

They said to each other,
"What is going on out there?
The noise is very loud.
We are very sleepy,
but there is too much noise
for us to sleep."

They waited
as long as they could stand it,
but the noise did not stop.
So the little girl
and the Queen of the Wild Horses
decided to fly out
into the dark, wet, noisy night
to find out
what was making all that noise.

Up and over the clouds
the night was not very dark,
and not wet, not at all,
but the noise was even louder.

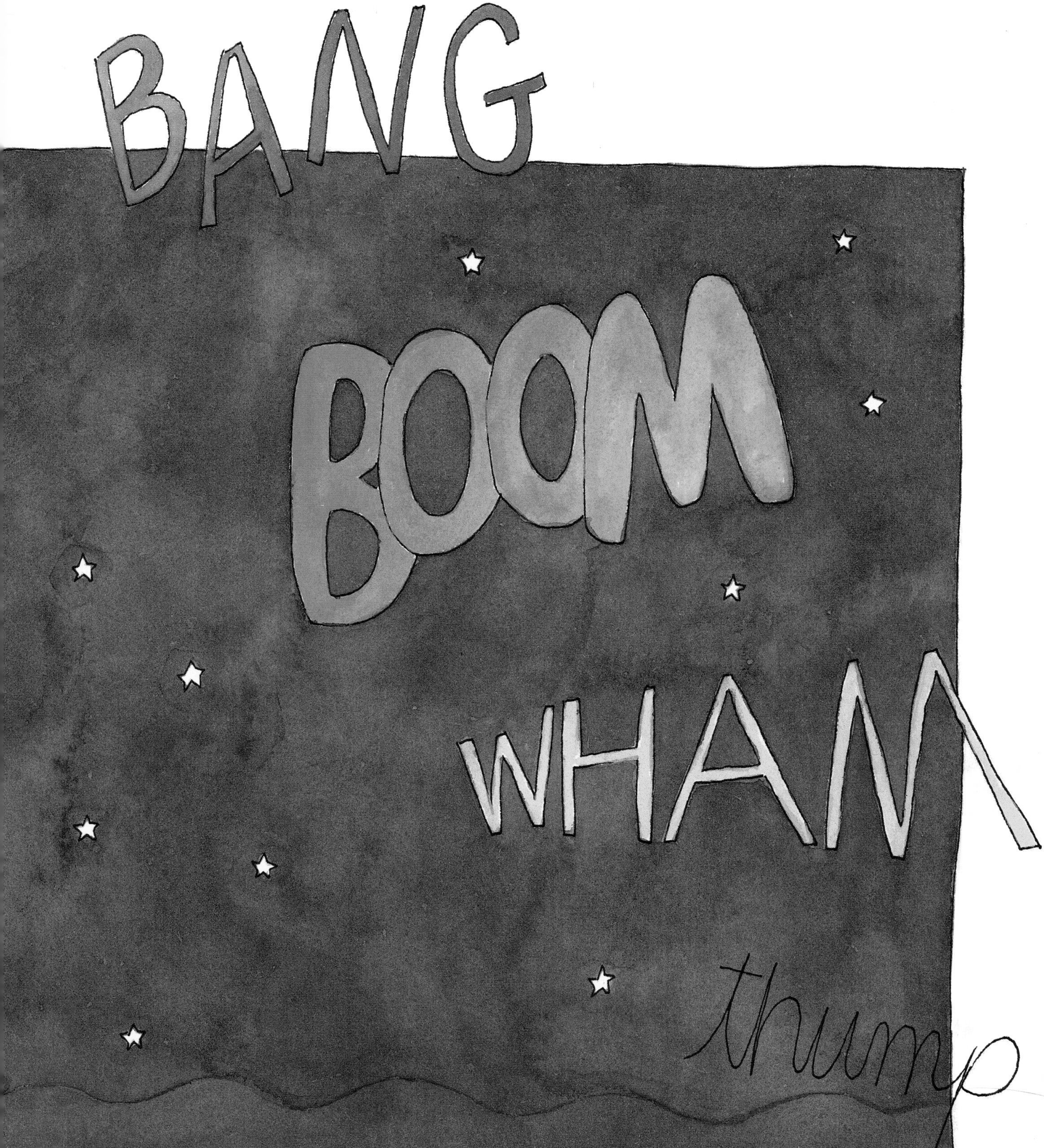
BANG
BOOM
WHAM
thump

Over the first cloud
they found
a crowd of dinosaurs
thrashing.

The Queen of the Wild Horses said,
"Hush, Dinosaurs. Please stop thrashing.
The noise is very loud.
This little girl is trying to sleep."

The crowd of dinosaurs yelled,
"NO.

"We will not stop thrashing.
We are thrashing because we cannot sleep.
We are very sleepy,
but there is too much noise
for us to sleep."

They listened.

BA WHUMP
BANG
BOOM
WHAM
thump

So they went on
to find out
what was making
all that noise.

Over the next cloud
they found
a herd of elephants
jumping.

The Queen of the Wild Horses
said,
"Hush, Elephants.
Please stop jumping.
The noise is very loud.
This little girl
and this crowd of dinosaurs
are trying to sleep."

The herd of elephants shouted,
"NO.

"We will not stop jumping.
We are jumping because we cannot sleep.
We are very sleepy,
but there is too much noise for us to sleep."

They listened.

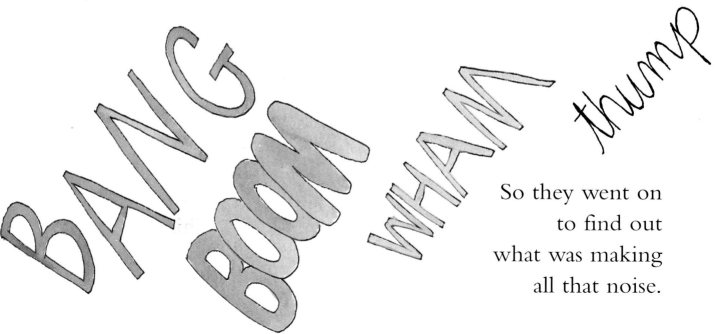

BANG BOOM WHAM thump

So they went on
to find out
what was making
all that noise.

Over the next cloud
they found
a gang of elk
bumping.

Over the next cloud
they found
a sloth of bears
bouncing.

BOOM BOOM

BOOM

Over the next cloud
they found
a bunch of beavers
slapping.

WHAM
WHAM
WHAM
WHAM
WHAM
WHAM
WHAM

And every time
the Queen of the Wild Horses
asked them
please to be quiet.

And every time
they screeched
and bellowed
and
howled,
"NO. NO. NO.

NO

NO

NO

"The noise is very loud.
We will NOT stop.
There is too much noise
for us to sleep."

The crowd of dinosaurs
and
the herd of elephants
and
the gang of elk
and
the sloth of bears
and
the bunch of beavers
and
the little girl
and
the Queen of the Wild Horses
all
listened.

There was still a noise—

thump

So they went on
to find out
what was making
that noise.

Over the last cloud
one little rabbit was thumping.

 *thump*

All of the animals
looked at the rabbit.
Its head hung down,
and its ears flopped,
and its eyes almost closed—
but it was still thumping.

thump *thump* *thump*

The Queen of the Wild Horses
said,
"Oh, please, Little Rabbit,
stop thumping.
This little girl
and this bunch of beavers
and this sloth of bears
and this gang of elk
and this herd of elephants
and this crowd of dinosaurs
are very sleepy,
but they cannot get to sleep
because you are making
too much noise."

thump

The rabbit
yawned
and cried,
"NO!
If I stop thumping,
I will fall asleep.
Everyone else is awake.
I am making noise
to keep myself awake, too.

"But I am very sleepy,
and if everyone will stop
thrashing
and jumping
and bumping
and bouncing
and slapping
and go to sleep,
then
yes,
I will stop thumping.

"YES.
Of course I will stop thumping.
Then yes,
I will stop thumping
right now."

The Queen of the Wild Horses
said to the animals,

"Will you please
stop making all that noise,
so this rabbit can stop thumping,
so this little girl
and this little rabbit
and all of you
can go to sleep?"

The dinosaurs yawned
"Yes"
and stopped thrashing
and sailed off to sleep.

And the elephants yawned
"Yes"
and stopped jumping
and floated off to sleep.

And the elk yawned
"Yes"
and stopped bumping
and glided off to sleep.

And the bears yawned
"Yes"
and stopped bouncing
and drifted off to sleep.

And the beavers yawned
"Yes"
and stopped slapping
and slipped off to sleep.

The rabbit was too sleepy to yawn, and it sank into sleep

beside the other animals.

The night was very quiet,
and the night was very dark,
except for the light of the moon
through the clouds.

The little girl
and the Queen of the Wild Horses
said,
"Thank you,"
and flew back down
and under the clouds.

And back inside,
the little girl
and the Queen of the Wild Horses
smiled at each other

and went to sleep.